You Will Be My Friend!

Peter Brown

MY FRIEND!

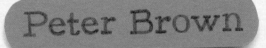
Peter Brown

MOM!
MOM!

SCHOLASTIC INC.

Lucy was very excited when she woke up.

MOM!
I've decided I'm going to make a new friend today!
Isn't that exciting?

That IS exciting, Lucille. But how do you plan on finding a new friend?

It didn't take long for Lucy to find another friendly-looking animal.

That friendship didn't work out either.

Lucy did her best to win over the forest animals.

She was helpful.

And she tried to fit in with everyone she met.

But Lucy was starting to feel ridiculous.

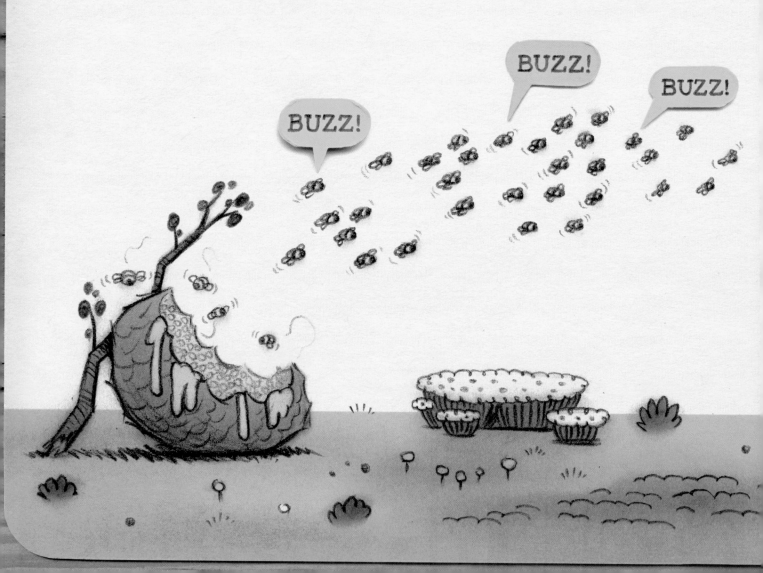

Lucy couldn't believe how hard it was to make a new friend. She was ready to be friends with ANYONE.

Well, almost anyone.

That's when things got ugly.

Lucy tried to calm
herself down.

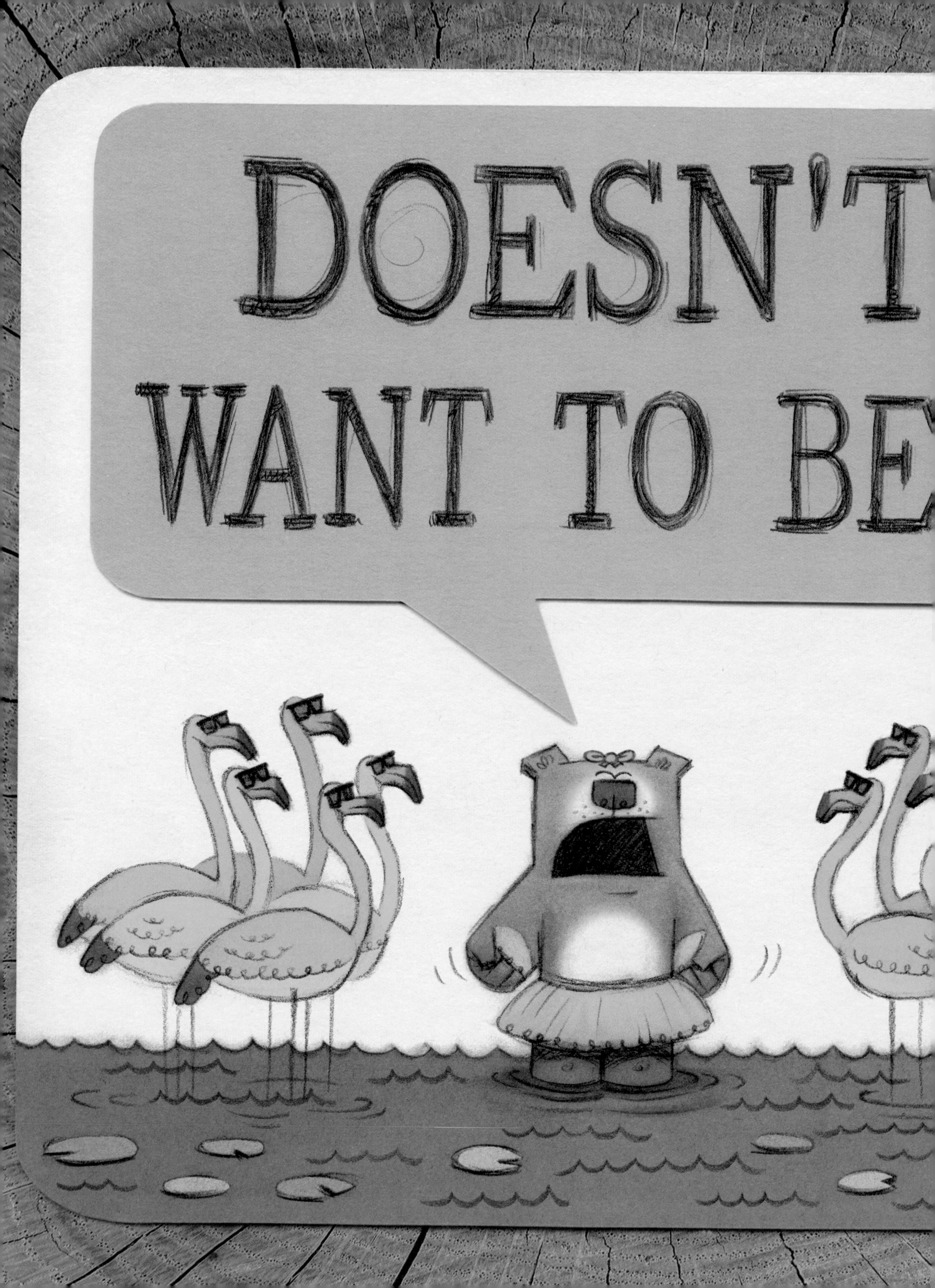
DOESN'T
WANT TO BE

It looked as if Lucy would never find a new friend.

And that's the story of how these two friends found each other.

The End